Belle and the Castle Puppy

Disney PRESS

New York

BELLE WAS STROLLING THROUGH the castle garden one chilly spring day, when she heard a whimpering sound. A shivering puppy was huddled by the castle gates.

"Oh, you poor thing!" Belle cried. "Let's get you warmed up and fed!" She wrapped the puppy in her red cloak and hurried to the castle kitchen.

The enchanted objects laughed when the puppy splashed in his bath. The dinner forks combed his fur while he gobbled a bowl of warm stew. Chip and his siblings giggled when he drank water from them.

"He's so cute! I hope we can keep him!" Chip said. But one enchanted object didn't join in the fun.

The ottoman watched the puppy. He remembered when he had been a real dog. Suddenly, he wanted some attention, too. With a funny little "grrr," he thumped around the kitchen, trying to act like the puppy. But no one noticed.

Just then, the puppy bounded to the door, barking eagerly.

"Do you want to go out to play?" Belle asked, opening the door.

As Belle and the others followed the puppy outside, they didn't see the ottoman slink out and wander off alone. They laughed as Belle threw sticks for the puppy to fetch.

Just then, the Beast walked up the path, clutching one of his precious rosebushes.

"Someone has dug up my roses!" he shouted.

Then the Beast saw the puppy. "Did that dog dig up my garden? Get rid of him—NOW!"

"I can't leave him in the woods," Belle argued. "He needs a home."

"He's not getting one here!" the Beast roared as he stomped away.

Belle knew that the Beast loved his roses, but what about the puppy?

Just then, the ottoman ran past Belle and the others. His legs were muddy.

"Ottoman dug up the garden!" Belle exclaimed.

"But why?" Lumiere asked.

As Belle watched the ottoman racing after the Beast, she suddenly understood.

"Oh, poor Ottoman," Belle said. "He just wanted some attention, too!"

Suddenly, the puppy raced after the ottoman, barking playfully.

Belle tried to call to them, but the ottoman and the puppy disappeared among the trees. "They'll get lost!" Belle exclaimed. "I have to bring them back safely."

"But it's getting dark," Mrs. Potts protested.

Belle looked at the long shadows creeping through the forest and shivered. Clutching her red cloak tightly, she took a deep breath and started toward the trees.

"Wait!" Lumiere called. "I'll come and light your way."

"Thank you," Belle said as she held the candelabra up high. "I'm glad you're coming."

"Me too. I think," Lumiere replied. But his flames flickered nervously.

"Puppy! Ottoman!" Belle called as she and Lumiere searched. Something rustled in the bushes. Yellow eyes gleamed at them.

"What is that?" Lumiere whispered.

"I hope it's just squirrels," Belle answered.

"They must be very big squirrels with very big eyes," Lumiere replied.

Belle picked up a large stick. Then she and Lumiere walked on, calling and calling.

Suddenly, they heard ferocious barking and snarling nearby. Belle ran toward the sound and stumbled into a clearing. The ottoman and the puppy stood under an enormous tree. Snarling wolves circled them. But the puppy was growling and snapping.

"He's protecting Ottoman!" Lumiere exclaimed.

"He's too small to stop those wolves for long," Belle answered. "He needs help!"

Quickly, Belle put Lumiere on the ground and lit her stick with his flames. Turning swiftly, Belle ran at the wolves, swinging the blazing stick at them.

"Get away! Get away!" she shouted.

Snarling angrily, the wolves backed away from the fire. Belle raced toward the ottoman and the puppy.

Just then, Belle tripped on a root. The torch flew from her hands.

"Oh, no!" she gasped.

The torch hit the ground and rolled just out of her reach. The growling wolves crept toward her.

Barking fiercely, the puppy raced to the flaming stick. He snatched one end in his teeth and darted among the wolves. As the wolves backed away, the ottoman ran in front of Belle, yapping for her to follow.

"The puppy's clearing the way!" Lumiere shouted to Belle. "Follow Ottoman!"

Suddenly, the Beast crashed into the clearing. The wolves scattered, yelping with fear.

The danger had passed. But the puppy's nose and ears were singed and sore.

"He and Ottoman tried to save me!" Belle said.

"They are brave little fellows," the Beast answered. Cradling the puppy in one arm and the ottoman in the other, he led Belle to the castle.

After the puppy had been cared for, everyone settled at the fireside. Belle watched the Beast stroke the ottoman and feed the puppy biscuits. The gentle smile on his face made her happy.

"May the puppy stay until I can find him a home?" she asked.

The Beast cleared his throat. "His home is here—with us," he answered gruffly. Belle smiled, knowing the Beast loved both of his pets dearly.

The next evening as Belle and the Beast waltzed in the ballroom, the puppy and the ottoman proudly kept guard at the door. Both wore shiny new badges. And on each badge were the words, PROTECTOR OF THE HOUSE.

Volume three of Disney Princess Classic Library

Printed in China

First Edition
1 3 5 7 9 10 8 6 4 2

T425-2382-5-12285
ISBN 978-1-4231-7937-5

For more Disney Press fun, visit www.disneybooks.com
This book was printed on paper created from a sustainable source.